Lights,
Action,
Land-Ho!

Lights, Action, Land-Ho!

JUDY DELTON

Illustrated by Alan Tiegreen

A YOUNG YEARLING BOOK

Published by
Dell Publishing
a division of
Bantam Doubleday Dell Publishing Group, Inc.
666 Fifth Avenue
New York, New York 10103

The trademark Yearling® is registered in the U.S. Patent and Trademark Office.
The trademark Dell® is registered in the U.S. Patent and Trademark Office.

ISBN: 0-440-40732-X

Printed in the United States of America

September 1992

10 9 8 7 6 5 4 3 2 1

CWO

For Sam Sebesta, my friend,
and my only fan with a bear rug
at the ready

Contents

CHAPTER 1

Movie Talk

"**S**chool's boring," moaned Roger White, throwing his math paper in the bushes on the way home.

"You're littering," said Tracy Barnes. "We got badges for not littering in Pee Wee Scouts."

"If I tell Mrs. Peters, she'll take your badge away," said Rachel Meyers.

"Will not," said Roger.

"Will too," said Rachel.

"Will not, will not, will not," said Roger, giving Rachel a shove off the sidewalk.

1

Kevin Moe scrambled into the bushes and picked up the paper.

It had lots of red check marks on it.

"Hey!" he shouted. "Roger got a *D* on this! He got only one right!"

Now Roger's face turned as red as the check marks.

"You're not bored in school, you're dumb," said Rachel, getting back at Roger for the shove.

"And you're a litterer besides," she called as she ran off down the street.

Molly Duff and Mary Beth Kelly caught up with her. They got to Molly's front steps, where they were safe, and sat down.

"Roger's right though," said Mary Beth. "School is boring sometimes."

"When's the next day off?" asked Molly.

The girls thought. It was October.

"Not till Halloween," sighed Mary Beth.

Rachel shook her head. "Columbus Day!" she said. "We have Columbus Day off."

"We should have a party for Columbus!" said Molly. "If it weren't for him, we wouldn't have a day off!"

Rachel snorted. "We wouldn't even be here," she said. "I mean, if he hadn't come to America, we would be living in England right now eating fish and chips."

"Or in Germany talking German," said Molly.

"And two Indians would be sitting right here on this front porch," Mary Beth pointed out.

"They had wigwams or lodges," said Molly. "There are no front porches on wigwams."

"And they really weren't Indians—they were Native Americans," she added. Molly had read up on Indians.

The girls thought about the Native Americans. Molly felt sad to think that her house replaced someone's wigwam. But she felt glad that she would have a day off from school soon.

"Columbus doesn't get much attention," said Molly.

"If he hadn't sailed to America, someone else would have," said Rachel. "In fact, a lot of other guys wanted to go discover it, but he beat them to it. They didn't have the money to buy a boat and stuff."

Rachel knew a lot, thought Molly.

"We can't even be really sure that Columbus did discover America," Rachel went on. "Historians disagree."

"Well, I know he did," said Mary Beth, standing up to go home. It looked to Molly like she didn't want to hear anyone bad-mouthing Columbus. After all, he was a national hero to some people. Children all over the country made little boats with puffy sails in kindergarten on his day. Would they do that if he hadn't really discovered America? And would all the schools close if he was fake? Molly wasn't sure.

"I have to go in," said Molly.

"We have Pee Wee Scouts tomorrow," said Mary Beth. "And I haven't got any good deeds to tell."

Rachel was still going on about someone else who was really in America before Columbus, but the girls ignored her.

"I'll ask my mom," said Rachel, "and I'll tell you tomorrow."

Molly went into the house to set the table for supper.

When her father came home from work, he cooked some corn on the cob. Mrs. Duff made hamburgers. They all sat down to eat.

"Do you know what I heard today?" said Molly's father. "I heard that a big company is coming here to our little town to make a movie."

"Really?" said Mrs. Duff. "I wonder why."

"I guess it's cheaper to make a movie outside of Hollywood," said Mr. Duff. "Maybe I'll go down and hang around. Maybe they'll put me in as an extra. What would you think of your old dad as a movie star, Molly?"

Mr. Duff posed like a movie star. Molly and her mother laughed.

"What's the name of the movie?" asked Molly.

"What's it about?" said Mrs. Duff.

Mr. Duff shrugged his shoulders. "I don't know," he said. "But we'll be finding out soon." He helped himself to another ear of corn.

"I'll bet Mrs. Peters knows," said Molly. "She knows everything that goes on around here."

Mrs. Peters was the Pee Wees' troop

leader. They all met at her house every Tuesday. Five boys and six girls.

The next afternoon after school, the Pee Wees raced to the meeting. They tumbled down the basement steps of Mrs. Peters's home and into their chairs around a big table. Nick, Mrs. Peters's baby, was sitting in a booster chair, banging on the table with a spoon. "Goo!" he said.

"Goo goo yourself," said Lisa Ronning.

Mrs. Peters came down the steps with chocolate cupcakes on a plate. Mrs. Stone, who was Sonny's mother, came down behind her with some milk. Mrs. Stone was married to the fire chief, who was Sonny's stepfather. She was also the assistant troop leader.

"Let's all take our seats!" said Mrs. Peters.

Roger picked up his chair and walked around the room with it.

"I'm taking my seat, Mrs. Peters," he said. "Where should I take it?"

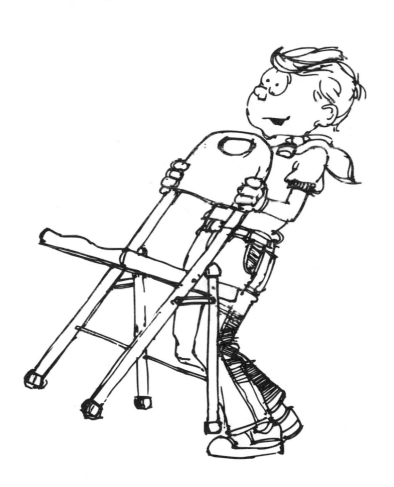

Everyone laughed.

"He's a smart aleck," said Kenny Baker.

"But he's funny," said Patty Baker, Kenny's twin. Patty liked Roger, thought Molly. She had made Roger a big red heart on Valentine's Day. Bigger than anyone else's.

Mrs. Peters ignored Roger. Molly was glad. Roger got too much attention.

"Let's sing our Pee Wee Scout song," she said. "And say our pledge. Then we will hear our good deeds. And *then*," she said with a smile, "I have a surprise."

The Pee Wees cheered. They loved surprises. Most of the time the surprise was fun. Once in a while it wasn't. Sometimes it was a lot of work.

"What do you think it is?" asked Tracy.

No one had any idea.

"Scouts are helpers, Scouts have fun," sang the Pee Wees to the tune of "Old MacDonald Had a Farm."

"Pee Wee, Pee Wee Scouts!
We sing and play when work is done,
Pee Wee, Pee Wee Scouts.

"With a good deed here,
And an errand there,
Here a hand, there a hand,
Everywhere a good hand.

"Scouts are helpers, Scouts have fun,
Pee Wee, Pee Wee Scouts!"

After the song, the Pee Wees said their pledge.

"We love our country
And our home,
Our school and neighbors too.

"As Pee Wee Scouts
We pledge our best
In everything we do."

"Now!" said Mrs. Peters, passing around the cupcakes.

Mrs. Stone poured the milk.

"Let's hear all the good deeds my Scouts have done."

Not many hands waved.

"I baby-sat my twins," shouted Sonny.

"He did not," whispered Mary Beth to Molly. "He can't take care of babies. I wouldn't trust him with my goldfish!"

Sonny was a baby all right, thought Molly.

"He probably means he sat with them while his mom was home," said Molly. She felt a little sorry for Sonny. Everyone laughed at him, and it was no fun to be laughed at.

"I dried dishes," said Tim Noon.

"Wonderful, Tim," said Mrs. Peters. "And Sonny," she added.

"Let's get on with the surprise," shouted Roger.

12

"That will keep," said their leader. "First things first. And good deeds are first."

Molly didn't want to think about good deeds. She wanted to think about the surprise. So did everyone else. But Mrs. Peters was not going to talk about the surprise till she got lots of good deeds.

Molly waved her hand.

"I took the smallest piece of cake on the plate when we had company," she said.

"That's good manners," whispered Rachel, "not a good deed."

But Mrs. Peters looked as if she thought it was a good deed.

"I watered the lawn and washed my dad's car," said Kevin. "At the same time!"

Mrs. Peters frowned as she thought about that. Then she smiled when she was sure it was a real good deed.

"I filled my bike tires," boasted Sonny.

"What's a good deed about that?" asked Roger.

13

"I did it for my dad," said Sonny.

"Hey, it's your bike, dummy," said Roger.

The good deeds were going downhill, thought Molly. Some of the Pee Wees were inventing good deeds. Making them up. Mrs. Peters must have noticed, because she said, "Let's see if we can work harder on helping others next week. And now it's time for the surprise!"

Everyone sat up to listen.

"A movie is going to be filmed in our town," said Mrs. Peters. "And the director has asked for some of you to be in it!"

CHAPTER 2

Star Struck

The Pee Wees were speechless. They stared at Mrs. Peters. Then they got their voices back.

"A real movie?" asked Patty.

"Can I be in it, Mrs. Peters?" asked Rachel.

"What's the movie about?" asked Kevin.

"What's the name of it?" asked Mary Beth.

"I'm going to be a movie star!" breathed Molly ecstatically.

"You don't know that *you* are in it," scoffed Roger. "She said some of us."

"Which some of us?" asked Tim.

"Me, me!" begged Lisa. "Can I be in it, Mrs. Peters?"

Mrs. Peters held her hand up for silence.

"I don't know much about it yet," she said. "I don't know the name of it or what it's to be about."

Rat's knees. Molly was disappointed in their leader. She usually knew everything. She could find out things Molly's own father couldn't find out.

"The director has just requested some Pee Wee Scouts for some of the scenes, but we won't know for a few weeks what the details are. The movie won't come out until next year. Then we will see it in movie theaters."

The Pee Wees shivered with excitement thinking about appearing in movie theaters all over the country.

"Is it for sure, Mrs. Peters?" asked Rachel.

"I mean, should we be rehearsing or anything?"

Mrs. Peters laughed. "I guess you can just think about putting your best foot forward," she said.

The rest of the meeting was boring to the Pee Wees. Nothing they could do and nothing their leader could say would top this news!

When Mrs. Peters talked about the park cleanup day, no one cared.

When she said, "Next week we are going to collect autumn leaves and label them," no one heard her. Molly was imagining herself in the movies with Kevin as the leading man. Would it be a love story? Would it be a song-and-dance musical? Maybe it would be a western! Molly could ride a horse. She even had a badge for staying on a horse in the rodeo parade.

Roger and Tim were pretending to fight a duel with swords.

Rachel was tapping a tune under the table with her foot.

"To be or not to be!" said Kevin. "That's Shakespeare," he said. "I could say that stuff in the movie."

Mrs. Peters tapped on the table.

"Let's say our pledge and go home," she said, laughing. "I can see we won't get anything else done today."

On the way home, Mary Beth said, "I'm going to get my Halloween costumes out. Maybe I can be a fairy princess in the movie."

"You can't wear a Halloween costume in a movie, dummy," said Roger. "They have real expensive stuff in the movies. Stuff with sparkling jewels sewn on."

"My costume sparkles," said Mary Beth.

"You don't know you'll be chosen," said Rachel with a toss of her head.

"Mrs. Peters said to put our best foot forward," said Molly.

"That means dancing," said Rachel. "You put your best foot forward when you tap-dance. And I've had four years of tap-dancing lessons. If we put our best foot forward, I'll be the one to get in the movie."

"Mrs. Peters didn't say whose best foot it would be," said Lisa. "We don't know it's you."

"I think putting your best foot forward means all of us," said Kevin. "I think it means we all have to get ready to show our talents off."

Kevin was smart. Probably the smartest boy in the Pee Wees. Molly decided she would listen to him. If she started now, she could learn to dance as well as Rachel!

When Molly got home, she ran to find her mother.

"Can I take tap-dancing lessons?" she asked.

Her mother frowned.

"You said you didn't want to take lessons

20

last spring when the class began," her mother reminded her. "The new class doesn't start till November."

Molly stamped her foot. November was too late. She had to learn now. And learn fast. She decided she would teach herself!

"I'm going to the library," she said, dashing out the door.

Molly didn't want to ask the librarian for help. Miss Brady might ask her why she wanted a dance book. And Molly did not want to explain. She didn't want anyone to know she was going to dance in the movie. Yet.

She wandered up and down the rows of books. She came to a sign that said HOW-TO. She read the titles of the books on the shelf.

How to Lose Ten Pounds.

Molly did not want to lose ten pounds.

How to Remodel a Kitchen.

Molly did not want to remodel her kitchen.

How to Be Your Own Best Friend.

Molly did not want to be her own best friend. She had a best friend. She just wanted to learn to tap-dance better than Rachel.

Finally she came to a book called *So You Want to Dance.*

She grabbed it. There were chapters on how to fox-trot. And how to waltz. The pictures showed ladies and men hanging on to each other and smiling. The ladies had long dresses on. The men had suits. She did not want a dance she had to do with a man. She did not want to waltz or fox-trot.

She put the book back and looked some more. She found a book about ballet. And right next to it was a book called *Tap-Dance Your Way to Fame.* Small letters underneath said Be the Life of the Party. Learn to Tap-Dance. Here was Molly's book! She hadn't thought about being the life of the party. But *fame* in the movies was definitely speaking to her. And if she happened to be the life of the party, too, it would be all right.

Molly took the book and checked it out on her library card.

"This is a two-week book, Molly," the librarian reminded her.

Molly nodded. That did not give her much time. She would have to spend every extra moment practicing! Could she be as good as Rachel in two weeks? She had to be.

When she got home, Molly went to her room and closed the door. She opened the book to the first lesson. There was a picture of someone in leotards with tap shoes on. Molly did not have leotards. She did not have tap shoes. She stamped her foot. How could she tap-dance with plain shoes?

Tap, tap, tap, she tried with her toe. But the sound it made was thud, thud, thud. Who ever heard of thud dancing? No, she needed shoes. Black patent leather shoes with bows you tie in the middle. With metal plates on the bottom. Putting your best foot forward was not easy. Molly sighed.

She remembered seeing a shoe catalog from Hanson's shoe store in her mother's room. She ran and got it.

"Supper's almost ready," called her mother.

Molly didn't want to eat. She wanted to dance!

In the catalog were lots of shoes. And slippers. And even rain boots. There was only one pair of tap shoes, on page 32. They were just what she wanted! Black and shiny! With a perky bow that tied in the middle! And big heavy taps on the heel and toe of each shoe.

Molly was all ready to call the store and order them. Then she noticed the price. $19.95. She shook her bank, which stood on her dresser. She emptied it out. When she added all the money up, it came to two dollars and forty-three cents.

She couldn't get a job—there wasn't time.

She couldn't ask her mother—it wasn't her birthday or Christmas. And $19.95 was too much for a no-occasion gift. After all, tap shoes were not practical. She couldn't wear them to school. She couldn't even wear them to church!

Molly would just have to find another way. And fast.

The next day after school, Mary Beth said, "I'm going to be a fairy princess in the movie."

"You have to do something, you can't just wear the costume," said Molly. Now she realized she would not only have to tap-dance better than Rachel, she'd have to be better than a fairy princess.

"I'm going to sing," said Mary Beth. "I'll be a fairy princess that sings."

The girls walked by Sonny's house. Sonny was on his front porch. Of all things, he was playing his old violin. Screech, screech, screech.

"Hey," called Mary Beth. "I thought you hated that thing. You didn't want to play it in the talent show last year."

Sonny played a very sour note.

"I'm going to be in that movie," he said as he ran the bow across the strings with a squealing noise.

The girls put their hands over their ears.

"Well, Sonny won't be any competition for us!" said Mary Beth.

"I'm going to tap-dance," said Molly as they walked on. "But don't tell anyone."

Mary Beth stopped. "Rachel tap-dances," she said. "Very well."

"I'm going to be better," said Molly crossly. "But I need tap shoes and I haven't got any money."

Mary Beth thought about that. She would have to help Molly. Her own talent was no problem. She already had the dress. And it

didn't cost anything to sing. Singing was free. All she had to do was open her mouth. Why didn't Molly choose something that didn't cost so much?

"Garage sales?" she asked Molly.

Molly shook her head. "They cost money too," she said.

The girls walked and thought some more.

Suddenly Mary Beth snapped her fingers.

"I've got it!" she said. "Leave it to me. I know how we can get tap shoes for you!"

Molly was glad she had confided in her friend. A problem always felt better when you shared it.

But Mary Beth had not said *where*. She had said *how*.

Was *how* to get shoes as good as *where*? She'd know soon.

CHAPTER **3**

Push Back Down

"I have to see your shoes," said Mary Beth. "Let's go look in your closet."

The girls ran to Molly's house. Molly threw open her closet door. Mary Beth took all the shoes out and lined them up on the floor.

"There are no tap shoes," said Molly. "I told you that."

"These are what I was looking for," said Mary Beth, holding up a pair of white Mary Janes.

"Those are white!" said Molly. "And they aren't patent leather. And besides, they're too small."

"Try them on," ordered Mary Beth.

Molly could just get them on, but they pinched her toes.

"They look fine," said Mary Beth. "We'll just paint them black and tie a bow where the buckle is!"

Molly looked doubtful. "They still won't tap," she said.

Mary Beth frowned.

"Unless . . ." said Molly. "We could glue taps on the bottom!"

"Of course," said Mary Beth. "That's what I thought. Where can we get taps?"

"I don't know where taps come from," said Molly. "But they are made out of metal, you know, like spoons or half-dollars or pie pans."

Mary Beth was thoughtful.

Then she said, "I think it's illegal to use

31

U.S. currency. And spoons are too small."

"Pie pans!" said Molly. "My mom has lots of extra pie pans!"

The girls dashed to the kitchen.

"Can I borrow some pie pans?" asked Molly politely.

"What for?" asked Mrs. Duff, who was studying her cookbook.

Molly paused. "For a surprise," she said.

Being the star of the movie would be a surprise for her mother, thought Molly. It was no lie.

"Sure," said Mrs. Duff, waving her hand toward the cupboard. "There are plenty of them in there."

Molly took two of the pie pans. She and Mary Beth ran down the basement steps and looked on the workbench shelf for some black paint.

"Here is some!" said Molly. She took the can and the little brush beside it.

"We need some strong glue," said Mary Beth.

Molly found some in the drawer.

HOUSEHOLD CEMENT, it said on the tube. HOLDS ONE THOUSAND POUNDS. BONDS ANY HOUSEHOLD ITEM EXCEPT CLOTH.

"We aren't gluing cloth," said Molly.

The girls ran upstairs to Molly's room. Molly put down some old notebook paper so that they wouldn't drip paint on the floor.

"Oooh, this is good!" said Mary Beth when Molly had painted the first shoe. "It's just right."

Molly looked at the black shoe. It didn't shine. But it was definitely black. She painted the other one.

"Have you got any hair ribbons?" asked Mary Beth.

Molly opened her dresser drawer.

"Not black," she said. "I don't have any black clothes."

"Let's use these," said Mary Beth. She held up some pink ones. "We can paint them black."

Mary Beth tied the pink ribbons on the black shoes.

Then Molly painted them black.

"They kind of droop," said Molly.

"That's because they are wet," said her friend. "They'll be okay when they dry."

The girls put the cover on the paint. Then they waited for the paint to dry. Molly blew on the shoes to make them dry faster like her mother blew on her fingernails when she polished them.

"Now for the important part," said Molly. "We have to glue the taps on."

"The pie pans look a little big," said Mary Beth.

Molly set one shoe in the pie pan.

Mary Beth was right. The pan was way bigger than a regular tap.

"That's okay," said Mary Beth. "Most tap

shoes have a little tiny tap on the toe, and a little tiny one on the heel! These will be much better, because they'll have metal on the bottom of the whole shoe! It will sound much better than other tap shoes," she added. "Better than Rachel's."

What Mary Beth said surely made sense. The more metal on tap shoes the better. The more tapping noise the shoes made the better.

"Squeeze out the glue!" said Mary Beth.

Molly did. She squeezed lots and lots of household cement onto the pie pans. Then she set each shoe in the puddle of glue.

"I don't like the way the pan shows around the shoes," said Molly.

"Pooh," said Mary Beth, waving her fear away. "When you are dancing, you won't notice that. You'll just see the silver sparkle."

"Let's practice together," said Mary Beth. "You need music, and I'm going to sing."

"These have to dry overnight," said Molly.

"Tomorrow after school," said Mary Beth.

When Molly woke up in the morning, the black paint was dry.

The glue was hard. The taps stayed on the shoes. She put them in a bag to take to Mary Beth's after school. She put her library book in the bag too. What would she wear to dance? Rachel had tights and little costumes. Molly looked in her closet. The closest thing she saw was some pajama bottoms. She'd take those. And she'd wear a blouse on top. Molly stuffed it all into a bag.

"I'm going over to Mary Beth's after school," she called to her mother on her way out the door.

"Be home for supper," called her mother.

At school all the Pee Wees were talking about being movie stars.

37

"I can play the violin really good now," said Sonny to Molly.

Roger heard it and snickered. "Ho ho ho," he said. "I'll bet."

Sonny stuck his tongue out at Roger.

Kevin was still quoting Shakespeare.

Roger had a magic set in his desk.

Lisa and Tracy and Patty said they were going to juggle plates in the movie.

Rachel was tap-tap-tapping her toes under her desk. Even with her school shoes on it sounded good.

At three o'clock Molly took her bag and went home with Mary Beth. Mary Beth had lots of little brothers and sisters.

"We'll go out in the garage," she said. "There's a cement floor to tap on and we'll be all alone."

When they got there, Mary Beth put on her fairy princess costume and began to sing "America the Beautiful." Molly sat down on an old box and opened up her dance book.

"Anyone can learn to tap-dance," she read. "If you can tap your toes to music, or drum your fingers, you can dance."

Molly felt encouraged. She put on her tap shoes. They felt tight.

"Take off your socks," said Mary Beth.

Molly did. That felt better.

Mary Beth began to sing again.

Molly turned to lesson one. The warm-up.

"Shake your leg," it demanded. "Like a rag doll."

"Then shake the other one."

Molly did. "This is simple," she said.

"That's enough warm-up," said Mary Beth.

Molly turned to lesson two. "Stamp your foot so that your heel and toe hit the floor together."

Bang, bang, bang, went Molly. Then she did it with the other foot. Bang, bang, bang.

"I don't know why Rachel needed all

those lessons," said Mary Beth. "There's nothing to it."

Next, the book told Molly to clap her hands and stamp her foot.

Clap, stomp. Clap stomp. Clap stomp. Mary Beth sang and Molly clapped and stomped all over the garage floor in her pie pans.

"You should skip some lessons," said Mary Beth, "because you're so good."

Molly did. She went right to ball change.

She did what the book said, but she couldn't lift her foot at the same time the other foot tapped. The two pie pans caught on each other and Molly fell to the floor.

"I think I'll skip that lesson," said Molly. "I don't think Rachel did that one."

The next lesson was the shuffle step.

Push, back, down. Push, back, down.

The pie pans banged into each other again.

Molly reached down and tried to turn the

pie pans up on the sides of her shoes. They didn't want to bend. Rat's knees. She and Mary Beth both pushed and pulled. Finally they turned up a little.

Push, back, down. Push back down.

"I can do it!" shouted Molly.

"You look good!" said Mary Beth to her friend. "That's a great step!"

But the next lesson was trouble.

"I can't do a heel drop," cried Molly, "because my heel and toe are all in one. My shoe can't bend."

"Skip it," said Mary Beth. "You don't have to do every step. No one will know the difference."

Molly looked doubtful. But maybe Mary Beth was right.

Push back down, went Molly. Push back down.

"That's your best step!" said Mary Beth.

She broke into a round of "The Itsy-bitsy Spider."

Push back down. Push back down.

"We're a team!" cried Mary Beth. "We can do our things together!"

Molly sat down on the box. She was hot and tired. Her toes were pinched. Her pajama bottoms were dragging. And all she could do was one dance step.

Would they be a team? Would Mary Beth sing better than she could dance?

Would Rachel dance better than she could dance?

And if there was a badge for being in this movie, would she be able to get one?

CHAPTER 4

Columbus the Pirate

On Tuesday the Pee Wees dashed to their meeting after school.

"I hope we find out more about the movie," said Sonny. "I don't want to be playing this old violin for nothing."

"I don't mind tap dancing," said Rachel. "I do it anyway. It isn't any extra work to do it in the movie."

It was extra work for Molly. A lot of extra work.

If Mrs. Peters told them the movie was off, Molly wasn't sure she'd mind. But if it was on, she still wanted to be the star.

Mrs. Peters had colored paper in her hand. She waved it over her head.

"We all know what day is coming," she said.

"Movie day!" shouted Roger.

Mrs. Peters laughed. "And also Columbus Day! We are going to make boats today!"

Everyone groaned. They wanted to hear about the movie.

"I don't know much more about the movie yet," said their leader. "Those movie producers work slowly. I do know some of you will be in it. And I think it is about Christopher Columbus. It will come out on Columbus Day next year. To celebrate his anniversary. And the other thing I know is that there will be a badge for the people who are in it."

"An acting badge, Mrs. Peters?" asked Tim.

"Columbus?" shouted Roger. "How

45

can we juggle plates in a Columbus movie?"

"Yes, an acting badge," said Mrs. Peters.

"Did Columbus play the violin?" cried Sonny.

"They didn't even have violins then, dummy," said Roger.

"I can sing a Columbus song in the movie," Mary Beth whispered to Molly. "And you can wear a Columbus costume when you dance."

"I have a perfect hornpipe costume," said Rachel. "I'll dance my sailor dance. Columbus was a sailor, so I'm all ready."

Molly felt the urge to choke Rachel. She was always so smug. She always had the right thing at the right time. Molly wondered if she hated her. Hate was bad. But who could like a perfect person? Especially a perfect person who bragged?

The Pee Wees sang their song.

They said their pledge.

They told their good deeds.

They had chocolate cookies with M&Ms in them.

And then they settled down to make boat pictures.

Mrs. Peters showed them the picture she had made.

The three boats she had cut out and pasted onto the paper were in a straight line. They were on a wavy blue sea. Their sails were puffy.

Molly couldn't get her sails puffy. She couldn't get her waves to splash. They seemed to go backward.

"Look at Sonny's!" whispered Lisa. "He's got paste all over the paper."

Sonny's boats were full of paste. They were not in a line. They looked like they were sinking headfirst into the sea.

"Hey, man overboard!" shouted Roger when he saw it.

When everyone was through, Mrs. Peters held up Rachel's boats.

They were perfect. Her waves were drawn right. Her paste did not show. And her sails puffed out farther than anyone's.

"I did a little extra, Mrs. Peters," said Rachel. "I put some sailors on the deck. You know, Columbus had a crew of men on each boat."

Sure enough, there were sailors on Rachel's boats. And letters on the boats saying their names.

Niña, Pinta, Santa Maria. Even Mrs. Peters didn't have the names on her boats. And she didn't have any sailors.

"Good for you, Rachel. It is always nice to add something creative to a picture, isn't it, Scouts?" said Mrs. Peters.

No one answered. They all wished that their leader had held up their pictures instead of Rachel's.

"I can't wait for the movie men to come," said Patty to Mary Beth.

"We can't either," said Mary Beth. "Molly and I have a team act. You should come and see it."

"I'll come and see it," said Rachel.

"Come over to my garage after school tomorrow," said Mary Beth. "Molly really is good."

"Okay," said Rachel. Some of the others said they would come too.

"Why did you say that?" asked Molly crossly. "I don't want Rachel to steal my dance."

There were other reasons Molly didn't want to dance for the Pee Wees. She had a feeling they might laugh at her pie pans. She knew the movie men would think it was a good idea, but the Pee Wees weren't that smart. They might think it was a dumb idea.

When the meeting was over, the Pee Wees

cleaned up and washed the paste off their hands.

"See you next week!" called Mrs. Peters. "By that time I'll have heard from the producers. Just get ready to be in the movies!"

"We are, Mrs. Peters," said Rachel.

On the way home, Molly said, "What can I wear to dance in? I can't be a sailor, Rachel's going to be a sailor!"

"You could be a pirate," said Kenny.

"Columbus wasn't a pirate," said Molly.

"But he might have had pirates on his ships," said Kevin.

Kevin was smart. And Molly liked him. She wanted to marry Kevin someday. If he said there were pirates on Columbus's ships, there probably were.

"You could wear one of those patches over your eye and carry a sword," Kevin went on.

"I guess I could," said Molly.

Molly felt a little better when she got

home. A pirate costume would be easy to make. She could just tie a rope around each pajama leg.

And it was good news that she could get a badge for all this work! It wouldn't be for nothing. She would both be a movie star and get a badge.

That evening Molly found a black patch to put over one eye the way Kevin had said. She found a rag to tie around her head. And cord to tie around her pajama legs. She made a sword out of an old fly swatter.

After school the next afternoon Molly and Mary Beth ran over to the garage. They put on their costumes.

"Maybe Rachel isn't coming," said Molly to Mary Beth.

But just as she said that, Rachel came up the driveway. She had on her sailor outfit. Little blue shorts and a blue-and-white shirt with an anchor on it. She had a little round white sailor hat on her head. Around her neck she had a whistle. And on her feet were tap shoes. Real, honest-to-goodness black shiny tap shoes with perky bows. They had real, honest-to-goodness metal taps on the toes and on the heels. And the shoes bent when Rachel walked. Tap, tap, tap they sounded as she walked up the driveway.

"Where do I sit to watch?" she asked.

Molly pointed to a box.

Before long Patty and Kenny came in, too, to watch. They sat on some old camp stools Mary Beth unfolded.

Rachel stared at Molly's feet.

"What are those?" she said.

"They're taps," said Molly. "The kind that cover my whole shoes."

Rachel did not laugh. She just shook her head side to side. Patty and Kenny sat politely on the camp stools and did not laugh either.

Molly took one last look at her book, and

waited for Mary Beth to sing. Then she began to dance, waving her fly swatter to keep
her balance.

Push back down. Push back down. Push
back down.

Rachel held her hands over her ears.

"You need music to dance," she said, in-
terrupting Molly's dance.

"What do you think this is, chicken
feed?" asked Mary Beth impatiently.

"You need real music. Dance music," said
Rachel. "It has to have rhythm and a beat."

Beat, schmeat, thought Molly. She bet Rachel couldn't do push back down as well as
she could.

Rachel stood up with her hands on her
hips.

"*This* is the way you do the shuffle step,"
she said, and with her hat bobbing she did
the push back down right across the whole
garage floor and out the door.

"That's shuffle off to Buffalo," she said,

54

coming back in. Molly wished she had shuffled off to the real Buffalo, instead of returning.

"I shouldn't really be dancing on a cement floor," she said. "It can ruin my taps."

Why didn't she go home then, thought Molly, and dance on her precious wooden floor and leave Molly alone.

"You have to move when you do the shuffle step," said Rachel. "This is the heel drop," she said, demonstrating.

Rachel's shoes bent just right to do the heel drop Molly could not do with her pie pans.

Rachel went on to show them what she called the four-tap cramp roll and some flaps and clicks. Then she did a chug, a brush step hop, and ended by making what she announced as an X turn and an O turn, ending up in a little twirl and bow, holding her hat up over her head.

"It would be better if there was music," she said.

"Hey, I thought this was Molly and Mary Beth's show," called Kenny.

"You do it now," said Rachel, full of encouragement. She gave Molly a little push. Molly wanted to punch Rachel for showing off. She wanted to take off her pinching pie-pan shoes and run home. But she couldn't. She couldn't admit Rachel was better than she was.

Push, brush, step, hop. Push, brush, step, hop, tried Molly. But it wasn't like Rachel's.

Rachel demonstrated again, making crisp clicking and tapping noises with her feet. There were lots of clicks and lots of hops and Rachel's feet were in the air one moment and tapping like crazy the next.

Molly tried to follow. Her heel had a blister and her toe had a cramp. Her pie pans went clank, clank, clank, instead of tap and click.

She tried a brush step hop and fell over.

"Well," sighed Rachel, putting her hat back on. "I'd better go and let you get a little practice."

She brushed off her silver taps and the tops of her shiny shoes with a paper hankie from her pocket. Then she retied her sailor scarf around her neck and shuffled off to Buffalo all the way down the driveway. The sharp, fast, musical sound of her taps made music in Molly's ears.

There was a lot of work to do before Molly was a movie star. Mrs. Peters said to be ready to be in the movies by next week. But even a week wasn't enough time to catch up with Rachel, thought Molly. Tears came rushing to her eyes. She had to admit, it looked like Smarty-pants Rachel might be the movie star instead of Molly.

CHAPTER 5

Only Extras!

Molly ran home and shut herself in her room. Maybe she should forget about tap dancing. About being a star. About competing with Rachel.

She kicked her tap shoes into a corner and lay down on her bed. She couldn't do that. She couldn't give up! Her dad always said, No one likes a quitter. Molly would be a quitter if she gave up. If she let someone else be the star!

Molly got up and put on her tap shoes.

Push back down. Push back down. Push back down.

She practiced for so long that her mother knocked on her door and wanted to know what was making all the noise in there.

"It's time for supper, Molly," she said.

Molly gobbled down her supper and ran back to her room to practice.

Push back down. Push back down.

By bedtime she had practiced a long time. But she did not seem to be any better at tap dancing.

"Rat's knees! Mrs. Peters always says, Practice makes perfect," shouted Molly to no one. "Well, it doesn't!"

Molly kicked off the tap shoes again and got into bed.

The next day was Tuesday. It was the Pee Wee Scouts meeting day.

"I hope Mrs. Peters knows who is going to be in this thing," said Sonny. "My arm is getting sore from practicing that darn violin."

"Did you ever hear of Columbus playing the fiddle?" whispered Mary Beth to Molly. "Sonny won't get chosen."

The Pee Wees sat around the big table in the basement. They sang and they recited, but their hearts weren't in it. They wanted movie talk. Lots of it.

"I didn't write in books," said Tim Noon when Mrs. Peters asked for good deeds.

Rachel waved her hand. "Mrs. Peters, it isn't a good deed not to do something bad. If he gets to use that good deed, then I can say I didn't talk back to my mother."

"And I didn't fight on the playground," said Kevin.

"I didn't set the house on fire!" laughed Roger.

"I didn't steal any candy," called Tracy.

Mrs. Peters held up her hands. She frowned. She had a problem here, thought Molly.

"Rachel is right. Good deeds should be

something positive," said Mrs. Peters thoughtfully.

Rachel said "Ha!" to Tim.

"But of course, if you have a bad habit and stop," she went on, "it may be a good deed."

All the Scouts began to talk at once. They all told about things they used to do but didn't anymore.

"I don't wake my little sister up anymore," said Mary Beth.

"I used to break dishes when I dried them," said Molly.

"When I was little I used to want the light on in my bedroom at night," said Patty. "I don't anymore."

Mrs. Peters held up her hand again.

"We will just have the good things we do for others," said Mrs. Peters. "Not things we don't do."

The Pee Wees settled down. No one raised a hand. It was easier not to do something than it was to do something, thought Molly.

"And now," said Mrs. Peters, "I have lots of movie news!"

"At last!" said Tracy.

Everyone sat up to listen. Now they would know who was going to be in the movie. Who was going to be a star!

Molly crossed her fingers. If she got chosen and Rachel didn't, she wouldn't have to worry about Rachel being better!

Mrs. Peters smiled. "You will like my news," she said. "Because the news is that all of you are going to be in it!"

Half the Pee Wees cheered. The other half booed. How could everyone be a star? thought Molly.

"The director told me he can use all of you as extras! So you all will be walk-ons."

"What does she mean, walk-ons?" asked Lisa. "Of course we have to walk on, unless we ride a horse!"

"A walk-on part," Mrs. Peters went on, "means that you all will be in the background. You will be in the group scenes. You will be part of a mob."

"Like the Mafia?" yelled Roger.

Background did not sound like a good word to Molly. It did not sound like something a star did. A star was up in front. Not in the back.

"Many stars are discovered this way," said Mrs. Peters. "They started out in mob scenes, and a talent scout discovered them and made them a star."

So there was hope. But there was no chance to be the star in this movie.

"Rat's knees!" said Molly to Mary Beth. "None of us can be a star."

"But there will be talent scouts there," said Rachel. "If we do well in the background, they might discover us. Me," she added, tossing her hair.

"Who do we get to be?" asked Mary Beth.

65

"The movie is about a modern-day town's celebration of Columbus Day, so the moviemakers want you to pretend to be modern children dressed as Native Americans.

"Remember, when Columbus came to America the Native Americans were already living here," their leader went on. "Columbus called the Native Americans 'Indians' because he thought he was in India."

"We are going to be Indians?" shouted Roger. "Yeah!"

Indians! Molly thought being an Indian would be exciting. She imagined herself wearing beautiful colored feathers. It would be fun. But it would not be stardom.

"Who gets to be Columbus?" shouted Roger.

"I'll bet it's some guy older than us," said Sonny.

"Columbus and all the rest of the cast will be played by Hollywood stars," said Mrs.

Peters. "Moviemakers bring along their own cast, and just use local people for the walk-ons."

Well. Instead of a pirate's outfit, Molly would need an Indian outfit.

"The producers will supply the costumes," said Mrs. Peters. "This is a professional movie, so they must be professional costumes. We must remember to do what the director asks, and be quiet and polite. We want to make the director glad that he or she asked the Pee Wees to have this honor."

"Yes, Mrs. Peters," said the Pee Wees.

On the way home, some of the Pee Wees grumbled.

But some were happy.

"I like being an Indian," said Tim.

"I don't like being in the background," said Sonny. "I want to be the star."

"Well, none of us are going to be the stars," snapped Rachel. "So get it out of

67

your head. You're just pretending to be an Indian like all the rest of us."

Molly did not want to be just a walk-on. She had a secret plan of her own up her sleeve.

The next day a big truck pulled up in front of Mrs. Peters's house. Two women and one man stepped out. Hollywood was here! thought Molly. But they weren't wearing dark sunglasses.

"They're here to measure you Pee Wees for your costumes," said Mrs. Peters.

"I think I have all of your sizes in stock," said the man. He brought out the costumes from the truck.

"They are beautiful!" said Rachel.

They were, thought Molly. They had colored beads sewn all over them. They looked like real leather. They had feathers. And fringe! They were the best costumes Molly had ever seen!

When all the Pee Wees had them on, they ran around the table chasing each other and whooping. Mrs. Peters frowned. She held up her hand. The Indians sat down.

"We will have several rehearsals," said one of the Hollywood women. "We rehearse without the walk-ons until production time, then we will include all of you."

She told them how to come onto the set. And how to walk. And how to act naturally.

"Don't stay in one big group," she said. "Spread yourselves around near the trees and in the woods. Pretend you are surprised to see Columbus arrive."

The Pee Wees nodded.

"Next Saturday they film!" said Mrs. Peters. "A van will take you out to Olsen's Woods. Be sure to be here at eight-thirty A.M. sharp!"

The Pee Wees were filled with excitement.

"Being an Indian isn't much different

from being a sailor," said Rachel. "Or a pirate."

"It's different from being a fairy princess," grumbled Mary Beth.

On Friday night Molly couldn't eat. She couldn't sleep. All she could think about was being in the movie.

In the morning, she was the first one at Mrs. Peters's house to get on the van. She had a small brown bag with her.

Rachel came next. She had a bag too.

"What's in there?" demanded Tracy.

"My lunch," said Rachel quickly.

"We get lunch on the set," Tracy reminded her.

"I might be allergic to it," said Rachel.

Sonny was carrying a big plastic bag when he came down the street.

Mrs. Peters was so busy counting noses of everyone on the van, she didn't ask any questions.

"All of you on!" she said. "We don't want to keep Hollywood waiting!"

That's right, thought Molly. It might be just walk-ons. But this was not pretend! This was really Hollywood!

CHAPTER **6**

Best Foot Forward

When the Pee Wees arrived, they saw cameras. Lots and lots of cameras. Men and women walked around looking busy. They all wore costumes. Columbus was there wearing big puffy pants.

"Where are the boats?" asked Molly. "Where are the *Niña* and *Pinta* and *Santa Maria*?" Molly was disappointed not to see them parked on the shore.

The Hollywood man who fitted their costumes said, "We don't film scenes on the boats here. We do that another day."

"It's not even real," scoffed Roger. "Having Columbus land before he sails!"

"That's the way movies are," said Rachel. "Scenes are not shot in order."

A friendly man named Sam, who looked like he loved to playact, said, "So here are our Pee Wee Scouts! Let's get you into costume and ready for Scene Three!"

The Scouts followed him to the dressing rooms, which were set up in the woods.

"There are no lights around this dressing table," whispered Mary Beth. "I thought movie stars' dressing rooms were fancier."

Sam laughed. "These are portable dressing rooms," he said. "We aren't as fancy when we are on location."

When the Pee Wees were in their costumes, Sam talked to them about Scene Three.

"The important thing is to just act natural," he said. "Laugh and talk, then pretend to be very surprised when Columbus and

74

his crew arrive. Maybe you are just a little bit afraid to see this stranger in your land. Remember, America is your land and these people have come uninvited."

There were lots of adult Native Americans milling about. Warriors with painted faces and feather headdresses. Indian princesses with black hair and beaded dresses. Old Indians smoking peace pipes. And one Indian papoose on a mother's back. Molly wondered if the real Native Americans had dressed like that all the time. She didn't think so. It would have been too hard to wash all that beaded clothing so often.

The Pee Wees milled around while they waited to be "shot." Mrs. Peters and Mrs. Stone kept counting them to see that no one ran off and got lost in the woods.

"I just hope a talent scout is here," said Rachel, looking around in the crowd.

"I hope so too," said Molly. This was her

chance to be a star. It was her *only* chance to be a star.

"Lots of stars get discovered doing walk-ons, my mom said," added Lisa. "I wonder what a talent scout looks like."

"Maybe like a Pee Wee Scout!" Kenny laughed.

Rachel was putting lipstick on her lips, Molly noticed. It was red and bright.

"My mom won't let me wear lipstick!" said Patty.

"This is special," said Rachel. "All stars wear lipstick. My mom lets me wear lipstick whenever I want to anyway."

"She does not," said Roger.

"Does too," said Rachel with a toss of her head.

Rat's knees, thought Molly. Why didn't she think to bring lipstick? Now Rachel would be discovered and she wouldn't!

Molly saw something red at the edge of the woods. It was a berry bush! Red berries grew on it. Here was her lipstick! She picked a few and rubbed them around the edge of her mouth. She decided not to put them on her whole lips because they might be poison. If they were poison and she got them in her mouth she might die, and then what good would it do to be discovered by a talent scout? She couldn't act if she was dead!

After she had put the red around her mouth, she decided to make her cheeks a little rosier too. She rubbed a little here. And a little there. Now she would look even better than Rachel. She had more than lipstick. She had real makeup.

She heard Sam call, "Scene Three, take one!" and took her little bag from the branch of a fir tree. She opened it and took out her pie-pan shoes. She slipped her moccasins off and her pie pans on. She ran out just as Sam called "Break a leg!" and winked at the Pee Wees.

The cameras began to roll. Columbus

walked in from the water onto the beach. He stopped to drop on his knees and kiss the ground.

"We are in India!" said Columbus to his crew. "And these people are Indians!"

The camera zoomed in on a close-up of Columbus, just as Molly came out of the woods doing a shuffle off to Buffalo. She shuffled right into a tree root and tripped and fell into Columbus's arms!

The Pee Wees looked shocked. The Indians looked shocked. Sam and the director looked shocked. But no one was as shocked as Molly.

"Rat's knees!" she said. "It is hard to tap-dance on grass."

"Cut!" called Sam, holding up his hand.

"What were you trying to do?" whispered Mary Beth. "And what's all over your face?"

Mrs. Peters dashed up and shouted, "First aid! Get a doctor! Molly has been hurt."

Mrs. Peters picked Molly up, pie pans and all, and carried her to a dressing room.

A doctor came rushing in.

"This child is bleeding," said Mrs. Peters.

The doctor put a cotton ball on the blood.

He began to laugh. "This isn't blood," he said. "It is some kind of juice!"

"It's makeup," said Molly.

Molly wished she could die. She was humiliated. Her first chance to be a star, and she failed. No talent scout would ever tap her on the shoulder and take her to Hollywood.

Sam helped her out of her pie pans and into her moccasins. Mrs. Peters scrubbed her face. It hurt. The berries had stained her skin.

"Now!" said Sam, laughing. "Let's try again! Everyone in their places."

"What a dumb thing to do," whispered Sonny. "You ruined the movie."

"Did not," said Molly. She hadn't ruined the movie. She had ruined her life.

"Scene Three, take two!" called Sam.

The Indians milled. Columbus fell to his knees again. He rose and walked toward the Pee Wees. He reached out his hand to shake the hand of the chief. Just as he did, who sailed past in her tap shoes and lipstick but Rachel! It wasn't easy to tap on the grass, but Rachel was doing it! Her taps flashed in the sunlight!

She danced right by Molly. And right by Columbus. When she got as far as the camera had panned, Sam yelled *"Cut!"* once more.

Mrs. Peters looked embarrassed.

Sam laughed. "Do we have any more tap dancers here today?" he asked. "Because if we do, we'd better see them now!"

The Pee Wees shook their heads.

"What a dumb thing to do," said Tracy.

"Anyone knows Indian kids didn't tap-dance in 1492."

Rachel did not seem to be embarrassed.

"We have to put our best foot forward," she said. "If there had been a talent scout here, I would be a star."

Mrs. Peters apologized and said there would be no more dancing.

"Take three!" shouted Sam. Columbus was beginning to look weary. But he fell to his knees and said "We are in India" for the third time.

This time he got to shake hands with the chief. He even began to smoke the peace pipe with him. Molly held her breath. It was one thing for her to try to be a star. She didn't want all the Pee Wees getting into the act.

Everyone relaxed as the camera filmed the Native American children playing in the woods. But they relaxed too soon.

All of a sudden, out of nowhere, as Columbus was eating some cornbread with the chief, there came a terrible sound. Flat, squeaky sounds blasted out of the woods.

"What is that?" shouted Kenny.

"I know what it is," whispered Mary Beth to Molly. "It's Sonny. He brought his violin."

"Cut!" shouted Sam. He did not seem as patient as he was earlier. Columbus threw himself to the ground in despair.

"I'll bet the director is sorry he ever hired the Pee Wee Scouts to be extras," said Tracy.

"I wouldn't ever do that," said Tim.

"That's because you don't have something to show off to be a star," snapped Rachel.

Mrs. Stone found Sonny and hauled him out of the woods. He was dragging his violin behind him. "I want to be a movie star," cried Sonny.

"To be or not to be," said Kevin, not

wanting to be the only one undiscovered. "That is the question."

Rachel snorted. "Shakespeare wasn't even *born* in 1492!" she said. "Kevin should know that. How could a Native American child say some lines that hadn't even been written yet?"

"It's time for lunch anyway," said Sam, looking at his watch. "Then we'll try again."

Mrs. Peters had a red face and tight lips. She did not look happy with the Pee Wees. Mrs. Stone looked angry too.

After lunch with the cast, Mrs. Peters took them aside and made it perfectly clear that no one was to do or say anything. Anything at all.

"You are just to stand around and pretend to be Native American children. Not dance, not sing, not play any instrument, not say any lines. You are to be in the background. Does everyone understand that?"

The Pee Wees nodded.

"You dummies," said Roger in disgust. "You wasted all the director's time and money."

"Did not," said Sonny.

"Did too," said Roger. "Didn't they, Mrs. Peters?"

But Mrs. Peters looked like she was afraid to say anything. For fear she would say too much.

"Take four!" called Sam, after lunch.

This time no one sang or danced or played the violin or said lines. Columbus dropped to his knees and got up and shook hands with the chief and smoked the peace pipe and ate cornbread. And the Indian children were angels. Columbus was the star. And the Pee Wees weren't.

CHAPTER 7

Molly the Star

"**H**urray!" shouted Columbus when Scene Three was finally filmed.

The Pee Wees changed back into their regular clothes. Mrs. Peters was still apologizing to the director for all the cuts.

"All's well that ends well," Sam said, laughing. "When the movie comes out next year on Columbus Day, the Pee Wees will be our guests at a big cast party."

"Maybe there will be a talent scout at the party," said Sonny. "I'm bringing my violin just in case."

Mrs. Peters and Mrs. Stone glared at Sonny.

"All right, all right, I won't," he said. "I'll sing instead."

All the cast laughed.

Molly wasn't laughing. She wondered what her parents would say when they found out she had tried to dance in the movie. And what about a badge? What kind would it be? Would she and Rachel and Sonny and Kevin get a badge after they had wasted the director's time and money?

Sam saw Molly brooding.

"It's all right," he said. "No one can blame you for wanting to be a star. Just practice more and come back later."

Was Sam telling her she still had a chance to be a dancer? Or even a movie star?

Molly thanked Sam and even gave him a little hug. He must think it wasn't too late for her to be a star! And everyone had to practice a lot to be successful. Why, look at

Columbus! He had to do scenes over and over to be a star. Molly shouldn't give up just because she failed this time!

On the way home, Molly sat with Rachel.

"I'm sorry I tried to be better than you," said Molly. "You are the one who should be a star. You really know how to dance and I don't."

Molly thought Rachel would say she knew that. That Molly was no good and she was. That she had talent and Molly didn't.

Instead, Rachel burst into tears. "I never get to play after school with the other kids because I have to practice so much. I have to go to lessons and practice all the time." She wiped her eyes.

Molly stared at her. Poor Rachel! Instead of riding bikes and playing ball, she was home practicing. Molly thought Rachel hadn't wanted to play with her. That she thought she was better than Molly. But it was because it was hard work to be best at something. She deserved to be best. To be a star. How could Molly expect to be as good as Rachel when she didn't have lessons before and she only practiced three times in her life?

Rachel turned to Molly and sniffed.

"If you really want to learn to tap-dance, I'll help you," she said. "You could come over to my house after school one afternoon every week and I could show you the steps. You could practice them at home."

"Really?" squeaked Molly. "You would really show me how to do it right?"

Rachel nodded.

"And I've got a pair of extra tap shoes you can have," said Rachel. "Real ones, black patent leather with bows. My mom got me new ones for the recital, but I didn't really need them."

Molly felt very warm toward Rachel. She went up to her and gave her a big hug. She may not be a very best friend like Mary Beth

was, but she wasn't as bad as Molly made her out to be. "Thanks," said Molly. "I'd love to learn those steps you do."

The bus pulled up at Mrs. Peters's house. Mrs. Peters looked tired, thought Molly. So did Mrs. Stone. It must not be easy to be a Scout leader. Molly felt sorry she caused so much trouble. But she hadn't known it was trouble when she did it. Who would think being a star would upset things so much?

When Molly got home, she told her mom and dad all about making the movie. She told them everything.

"Molly, my movie star," her father said.

"Not yet, but I'm going to be," she said. "I've still got lots of time."

"Speaking of time, it's time to do some homework," said her mother.

"No, it isn't," said Mr. Duff. "Because guess what day tomorrow is?"

Molly and her mother thought and thought.

"It's a free day!" said her dad. "Thanks to Christopher Columbus!"

Molly covered her ears as her dad said, "Columbus sailed the ocean blue in fourteen hundred ninety-two."

Maybe someday she would want to think about Columbus again. But right now she had Christopher Columbus overkill. She would have a good time with her friends on the free day and try not to think of Columbus once.

That evening Mrs. Peters called. "I'd like you to come over and watch the six o'clock news," she said. "There will be a surprise for all the Pee Wees!"

On the way, Molly met the other Pee Wees rushing over to Mrs. Peters's. When they got inside, a woman on TV was saying, "The Pee Wee Scouts were celebrities today."

"What's a celebrity?" whispered Tim.

The woman went on. "They helped make a Hollywood movie about Columbus, whose birthday we celebrate tomorrow. Our Pee Wees dressed up as Native American children."

As the announcer's voice boomed, pictures of the woods flashed onto the screen.

"That's Scene Three, take four!" cried Rachel.

"Look, there's my arm," shouted Tim.

"That's *my* arm, dummy," shouted Sonny.

Molly watched the Native American children flash onto the screen. She saw part of Mary Beth. And Roger's face. All of Rachel was there. But none of Molly! It looked like everyone was on the news but Molly!

When it was all over, Molly felt bad. Now she would never be famous.

Mrs. Peters's phone gave a loud ring. She went into the other room to answer it. When she came back, Mrs. Peters was smiling.

"That was Sam," she said. "The directors liked the noise that Molly's pie pans made. They want her to sign a release so that they can use the noise in other movies for things like thunder or broken dishes."

Molly couldn't believe her ears! So she wasn't on the news, and her pie pans would not show in the movie. But a talent scout had discovered her! The sound of her pie pans would be heard in movies!

"Molly's pie pans may make her famous yet!" Mrs. Peters said, laughing.

All the Scouts clapped and cheered. Wait till she told her parents this news! And on top of this she would learn real tap-dance steps from Rachel. And wear real tap-dance shoes. It was wonderful to be a Pee Wee Scout!

As the Pee Wees were ready to leave, Mrs. Peters called, "Be sure to be at our meeting on Tuesday! That is the day you will all be getting your acting badge!"

Mrs. Peters had used the word "all." That must mean that Molly would get her badge too.

Molly ran all the way home. She told her parents about the call from Sam.

"You are a star already," said her father, "and the movie isn't even out yet!"

Molly gave her parents a hug and went to her room. She had one more thing to do. She took her pie-pan shoes and carefully wrapped them up, then put them in her closet. She hoped her mom had more pie pans to use for pies, because these were ruined forever.

But it was a small price to pay for stardom!

Pee Wee Scout Song
(to the tune of "Old MacDonald Had a Farm")

Scouts are helpers, Scouts have fun
Pee Wee, Pee Wee Scouts!
We sing and play when work is done,
Pee Wee, Pee Wee Scouts!

With a good deed here,
And an errand there,
Here a hand, there a hand,
Everywhere a good hand.

Scouts are helpers, Scouts have fun,
Pee Wee, Pee Wee Scouts!

 **Pee Wee Scout Pledge.**

We love our country
And our home,
Our school and neighbors too.

As Pee Wee Scouts
We pledge our best
In everything we do.